Toot & Puddle

Charming Opal

by Holly Hobbie

LITTLE, BROWN AND COMPANY
New York • Boston

Little, Brown and Company

Hachette Book Group
237 Park Avenue, New York, NY 10017
Visit our website at www.lb-kids.com

Little, Brown and Company is a division of Hachette Book Group, Inc.
The Little, Brown name and logo are trademarks of Hachette Book Group, Inc.

First Paperback Edition: May 2011
First published in hardcover in September 2003 by Little, Brown and Company

Library of Congress Cataloging-in-Publication Data

Hobbie, Holly.
Toot and Puddle: Charming Opal / Holly Hobbie.
p. cm.
Summary: When his cousin Opal loses a tooth during a visit, Puddle dresses as the Tooth Fairy
so that Opal's hope of receiving a shiny quarter will not be disappointed.
ISBN 978-0-316-36633-5 (hc) / ISBN 978-0-316-12655-7 (pb)
[1. Tooth Fairy — Fiction. 2. Teeth — Fiction. 3. Cousins — Fiction.
4. Pigs — Fiction.] I. Title.
PZ7.H6517 Tq 2003

[E] — dc21   2002066097

10 9 8 7 6 5 4 3 2 1

SC

Printed in China

The paintings for this book were done in watercolor.
The text was set in Optima, and the display type was hand lettered.

For Jocelyn

In July Puddle's little cousin, Opal, came to Woodcock Pocket for a holiday.

On her first day Toot and Puddle took Opal for a long walk in the sparkling woods.

The three of them played with her new purple ball.

She smelled every flower in Puddle's garden.

That evening they had a cookout with corn on the cob and watermelon.

When Puddle was tucking Opal into bed, she said, "I love to come to Woodcock Pocket."

"We love to have you here," said Puddle. He added, "It looks like you're going to lose that tooth pretty soon."

"I know," Opal said proudly. "I can hardly wait."

At breakfast, Opal said, "Look, Toot,
my tooth is so WOBBLY."

"Would you like me to help it come out?" Toot asked.
Opal said, "I want it to come out all by itself."

They picked big, beautiful strawberries in the morning.

"I don't think that tooth can get any looser, Opal," Puddle said.

"It might fall out today," Opal said, laughing. "Right during my vacation at Woodcock Pocket."

In the afternoon they set off for Pocket Pond.

"Last one in is a rotten egg," Toot called, somersaulting into the water.

Puddle made sure Opal went second.

All at once Puddle noticed that Opal looked slightly different. "Holy moly," he said. "Your tooth!"

Yes, Opal's loose tooth had fallen out at last.

"But where is it?" Opal asked, looking anxiously at the ground. She was bravely trying not to cry.

"Why are you upset?" Puddle asked. "You've been hoping for your tooth to come out."

"But where is it?" Opal repeated. "I have to put it under my pillow tonight."

"You do?" asked Toot.

"So the Tooth Fairy will come," she explained.

"I see," said Puddle. "We'll have to find that loose tooth."

"That lost tooth!" Toot said.

They searched everywhere — along the path, and back at the house, and all around the pond — but Opal's tooth seemed to have vanished.

"It must have come out while you were in the water," Puddle decided.

"Then it's gone forever," his little cousin said sadly.

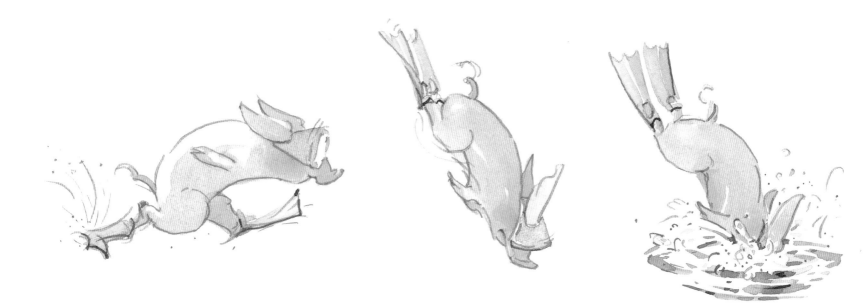

"Maybe not," shouted Toot.

Lo and behold, on his third dive Toot spotted Opal's white tooth on the sandy bottom of Pocket Pond.

As Puddle tucked his little cousin into bed that night, she carefully placed her tooth under her pillow. "Now the Tooth Fairy will come while I'm at Woodcock Pocket," she said, "just as I'd hoped."

"Sweet dreams," said Puddle.

But he was worried.

"What's the matter, Puds?" Toot asked.

"Do you think the Tooth Fairy comes to Woodcock Pocket?"

"I'm not sure," Toot said. "Maybe."

"But what if she doesn't? Opal will be so unhappy."

Puddle devised a plan. They would stay awake and make sure the Tooth Fairy visited Opal's bedroom. And if she didn't come to collect the precious tooth and leave a shiny new quarter in its place, Puddle would do the task himself. "I will be the Tooth Fairy," he declared.

"How do you be the Tooth Fairy?" Toot asked.

An hour later Puddle returned to the living room.

"I am the Tooth Fairy," he announced. "Am I believable?"

"Quite believable," Toot told him.

"Now let's turn out the lights and wait for the Tooth Fairy to arrive," Puddle said.

"Oh, no," said Puddle. "We both fell asleep."

"Did you hear anything during the night?" Toot asked.

"Not a sound," Puddle said. "Is it too late for me to be the Tooth Fairy?"

They heard Opal calling them from the other room.

"I'm afraid it is too late," said Toot.

Toot and Puddle stepped nervously into the guest bedroom.

"Good morning, Opal," they said together.

"I was thinking," Puddle began, "if the Tooth Fairy didn't come, it's because she didn't know exactly where Woodcock Pocket was, after all."

"And I was thinking," said Toot, "if the Tooth Fairy didn't come, it would be just as nice to keep that wonderful tooth of yours for yourself."

"But guess what?" Opal said. "The Tooth Fairy did come!"
Grinning happily, she held out a shiny new quarter for
Toot and Puddle to see.